CONTENTS

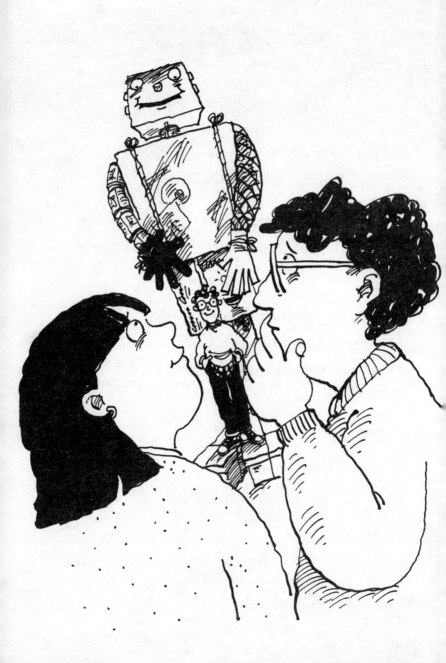

The Missing Monster

Written by Ann Jungman
Illustrated by Jan Smith

ORCHARD BOOKS

Other brilliant Frank N. Stein stories are:

The Monster Idea
Monster In Trouble
Monster In Love

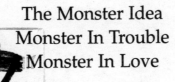

For Alex, with love
AJ

ORCHARD BOOKS
96 Leonard Street, London EC2A 4RH
Orchard Books Australia
14 Mars Road, Lane Cove, NSW 2066
ISBN 1 86039 144 3 (hardback)
ISBN 1 86039 362 4 (paperback)
First published in Great Britain in 1996
First paperback publication 1997
Text © Ann Jungman 1996
Illustrations © Jan Smith 1996

The Monster Hut

"Where we are going to put him I do not know," said Mr Stein with a sigh, looking at the huge monster his son Frank had made.

"I don't mind where I live," said the monster cheerfully, "just so long as I'm not too far from my boy Frank."

"He can't live in house," declared Mrs Stein. "That's for sure."

"Why not?" demanded the monster, looking tearful. "Don't you want me?"

Mrs Stein smiled and took the monster's big hand, "That's not it, silly. You can't get in through the doors, remember. You would bang your head on the ceiling. You've eaten so much rubbish you've grown."

The monster giggled. "That's right, I'm too big. I could live in the garage. I was

made in a garage, yes the garage would suit me fine."

"No!" yelled Mr Stein. "That's where I keep the car. Oh dear, I don't know what I did to deserve this problem."

"It's because you called me Frank Norman Stein," said his son quickly. "It's your own fault that you've got to find a home for a monster."

"I know," groaned his father. "We called you Frank after your mother's uncle, and Norman after my grandfather. We didn't realise it would lead to you being called

Frankenstein. We didn't think of it at the time."

"Good thing you didn't," chortled the monster, "or I wouldn't be here."

"I'm glad too," said Frank gazing affectionately at his monster. "I never thought I would ever say that I was glad that my name is Frank N. Stein – but I am."

The monster's eyes filled with tears. He picked Frank up and gave him a big hug.

Just then a team of TV reporters from America turned up and wanted to interview Frank and his monster.

"Could you tell our viewers just how this monster came into being please, Frank?"

Frank took a deep breath and then told his story into the TV camera.

"The kids at school teased me because my name sounds like Frankenstein, so a group of us built this monster out of bits and pieces. Then there was a huge thunder storm and he came alive. Luckily he turned out to be completely harmless – all he wants to do is eat rubbish. Isn't that right, monster?"

The monster beamed and waved. "It certainly is, my boy Frank. Eat rubbish, that's all I want to do." He grabbed the camera. For a terrible moment it looked as though he was about to swallow it whole.

"No!" yelled Frank and his parents and the interviewer together. The monster put the camera down and looked puzzled.

"Is something wrong, Frank?" he asked, shaking his big head.

"It's all right, Steinasaurus Rex," said Frank soothingly. "You just eat up some of these black sacks of rubbish and leave the camera alone."

"Is it true that Steinasaurus Rex is called after you, Frank?" asked the interviewer.

"Certainly is," said the monster, as he munched the final remains of the bag of rubbish. "After my boy Frank. That's me – Steinasaurus Rex."

"Is it right that this country no longer has a rubbish disposal problem?"

"Quite right," said Frank proudly.

"Yes," agreed the monster, "I'm never hungry and they don't have any problems with the rubbish. It suits everyone."

When the TV crew had gone, Mrs Stein looked at the monster and sighed.

"We'll have to build a big shed at the bottom of the garden," she said.

"Where?" demanded her husband.

"Where the vegetable patch is," said Frank's mother.

"But Mum," cried Frank. "You love growing all those lettuces and tomatoes and herbs."

"Yes I do," agreed Mrs Stein sadly. "But

the monster has to have somewhere to live and it has to be near you Frank, so that's the only solution as far as I can see."

"That's very kind of you, Frank's mum," said the monster. "Now show me where you are going to build my house."

So they walked down to the bottom of the garden, where the rows of lettuces were neatly laid out and the rhubarb and spinach were sprouting.

"Pity about your vegetable patch," said the monster. "Those tomatoes look so nice and fresh."

"Never mind," said Mrs Stein bravely "We can manage without."

The monster looked round and sniffed loudly. "I'll like it here. There are lots of nice trees and the birds singing. . . and

what's that lovely smell?"

"It's the compost," said Mrs Stein. "I'm so sorry, I forgot about that. We'll move it."

"No need to do that," cried the monster and ate the lot in two minutes.

"Very nice that was. You can keep on putting the compost down there. Then if I get peckish at night I can have a little nibble."

"Nibble!" shouted Mr Stein. "You've scoffed the lot. We use it to enrich the soil in the garden. It's not a snack for monsters."

"Don't worry about that dad," said Frank quickly. "We'll leave some rubbish near the monster's house and I'm sure he'll promise to leave the compost alone. Won't you Steinasaurus Rex?"

"S'pose so, if you say so Frank," grumbled the monster. "But that compost is very tasty, very tasty indeed."

Later that day a van from the Department of the Environment arrived with a wonderful wooden hut for the monster.

"It's very grand," commented Frank, as the workmen began to put the hut together in the garden.

"Of course," replied the foreman. "The Minister said that there was to be nothing but the best for Steinasaurus Rex because he is doing so much good for the country, eating all the rubbish and that."

The monster grinned and swelled up with pride. "Nothing but the best for me. Did you hear that Frank? "

"I did," nodded Frank N. Stein. "And I agree absolutely. Nothing but the best for my monster."

By the time the hut was finished it looked wonderful. In front of it were pots full of flowers. Each window had window boxes, and hanging baskets hung over the huge door. Nearby was dustbin full of rubbish with pots of sweet smelling flowers hanging from it.

"That's for me, if I get peckish in the night," the monster told the Steins.

"Oh no, all my lovely flowers will be trampled," said Mrs Stein. "Oh why didn't we call him Norman Frank, and then none of this would have happened!"

"I know dear," agreed Mr Stein, "but the monster does make Frank very happy."

The monster went on living happily at the bottom of the garden. Each day he would eat breakfast with Frank and then go wherever he was needed to eat rubbish.

That is until early one morning. Frank ran down to the hut as he always did, and found the hut empty.

"Monster!" yelled Frank. "Steinasaurus Rex come here this minute and stop messing around."

Frank ran round the garden calling out the monster's name. He looked in the neighbouring gardens and out in the street. But there was no sign of the monster anywhere.

Then Frank noticed that the flower pots were smashed and the window boxes broken. Frank felt a sinking feeling in his stomach.

"Steinasaurus Rex is missing! Oh dear, I hope it's just that he got bored and has gone looking for food. I hope he hasn't gone for good."

Missing

Frank tried not to panic. "He must have got hungry and gone for a walk that's all," he thought. "I hope he only eats rubbish and not anything valuable like a car. I'd better find him before anything awful happens."

He went in search of his friend. As Frank walked down the street he asked the milkman if he had seen a monster.

The milkman laughed, "Sorry son, the only monsters I've seen today have had a human form."

Frank was puzzled, if the monster was anywhere near surely the milkman would have seen him. Then the postman came round the corner.

"My monster's not in his shed," Frank told the postman. "Have you see him?"

"What the great big fellow I saw on TV?"

"That's him," said Frank.

"Oh no, I haven't seen anyone like that. I mean you couldn't miss him, could you?"

"I know," sighed Frank.

"I'd go and ring the police if I were you," suggested the postman. "Someone is sure to have reported him. I bet he's having the time of this life on some rubbish dump."

"Hope so," muttered Frank, "But it's not like him to go wandering off without me." And he walked home quickly.

As he went back into the house he heard his mum calling.

"Frank is that you?"

"Mum, my monster's disappeared. Have you heard anything?"

"Disappeared!" cried Mrs Stein. "Don't be silly Frank. How could a huge great thing like that just disappear?"

"I don't know mum," replied Frank, fighting back the tears, "but he has."

"I'll call the police," said Mrs Stein quickly. "Eat your breakfast while I phone."

Frank was too worried to eat. He stood beside his mother while she dialled the police station.

"What are they saying," he asked her. "Have they seen my monster? Do they know where he is?"

"Be quiet," hissed his mother. "I can't hear a word." And then she said, "Oh, so there haven't been any reports of sightings. How odd, how very odd. Yes, well please do keep us informed and we'll let you know if we hear anything. I expect there's a simple explanation. Yes, I'll be here all morning so when your people arrive to investigate I can let them in."

"Where can he be?" demanded Frank, pacing up and down. "I mean he can't just have disappeared into thin air. Maybe my monster decided he didn't like me after all and ran away."

"Oh Frank," said his mum, putting her arms round him. "Of course that isn't what happened. Now go and get ready for school."

"You must be joking," cried Frank. "I can't go to school while my monster is lost.

I've got to stay here in case he calls and needs me."

"No you can't just miss school," said his mother. "But I'll be here all day, and I promise you that if there's any news I'll let you know straight away."

For the whole of the morning Frank sat and looked out of the window. He didn't hear one word the teacher said.

At playtime, Jason, Chris, Achmed and Mark crowded around Frank.

"What's up?" they asked.

"I suppose you ought to know what's happened. You did help to build him. Steinasaurus Rex has disappeared."

"Disappeared!" echoed the boys.

"But that's not possible," cried Jason. "He's too big to disappear."

"I know," agreed Frank miserably. "But he has just disappeared."

The word soon got round that the monster was missing and none of the children did a jot of work that day.

After school, Frank and his friends raced back to Frank's house. The monster had not come back and there had not been any sightings. The police had been round but there were no clues of any kind. Frank was in despair.

That evening, all the children were glued to the television news. Their parents could hardly persuade them to go to bed. When they arrived at school the next day, each class had a radio on the teacher's desk.

"Because this is a special emergency," the headmaster told the children, "I have decided to have a news bulletin every half hour, but only on condition that you all do your work as usual."

The children cheered and every half hour the radio was switched on and you could have heard a pin drop. But there was no news of Steinasaurus Rex.

Interpol had been alerted. All airports, stations and ferry terminals were being watched.

Frank was deluged with letters and cards and telegrams of support from children all over the country. They all promised to look out for the monster and let Frank know if there was any sign of him. But in spite of the search, no one found a single trace of Steinasaurus Rex.

Frank couldn't eat he was so worried. Mr and Mrs Stein worried about Frank and the monster. No one knew what to do next.

Then one morning at breakfast Mrs Stein suddenly grabbed the daily paper and yelled, "Listen to this! 'After many years of silence there are rumblings again in Loch Ness. Nessie, the famous Loch Ness Monster, is said to be haunting the lochs of Scotland. Local residents claim to have seen and heard Nessie for the last eight nights.' Ha! This may be the breakthrough we've been waiting for."

Nessie or not?

"I don't see what Nessie has got to do with my monster," muttered Frank, staring gloomily into his glass of orange juice.

"Maybe nothing," said his father, "but this is the first mention of a monster since our dear old Steinasaurus Rex disappeared. Who knows – there may be a connection."

"Yes," agreed Mrs Stein, "And next week is half-term."

"Quite so." nodded her husband. "And we've been meaning to take a holiday in Scotland for years."

"And you're owed a week's holiday," finished Mrs Stein, "so I will go into the travel agent this morning and book us a week in Scotland on Loch Ness."

"But what if my monster wants to get in touch?" demanded Frank. "He might think that we've abandoned him. I don't think this is a good time to go away."

"No problem," said his mother firmly. "We'll arrange to have the phone manned twenty-four hours a day. So many people want to help, they can take it in turns."

"Remember the police are watching the house and monitoring all phone calls," added his father.

"I'd still rather be here," grumbled Frank.

"Nonsense," said his father briskly, "I've got a gut feeling that these sightings of Nessie and the disappearance of our monster are linked."

A few days later the Steins were on a coach, looking out at the glorious Scottish scenery.

"Look," cried Mr Stein, "Loch Ness."

"I can't see anything like a monster," said Frank sadly.

"I know," agreed his mother. "And definitely nothing like our monster."

"Give it time, you two," said Mr Stein, getting their bags down from the rack. "Give it time."

Before long the Steins were settled in their hotel room.

"Let's go for a walk and talk to the locals," said Mum.

"Yes," agreed Mr Stein enthusiastically. "Maybe we can glean some information about this mysterious appearance of Nessie, the Loch Ness Monster."

Frank beamed at his parents.

"I think you really like my monster too," he said.

"Well yes," said his mother. "Even though he has ruined my lovely vegetable patch."

The Steins walked along the side of the loch. They admired the rolling hills and the smooth outlines of the water, and then went to have tea at the café.

"Did anyone here see the Loch Ness monster?" asked Mr Stein.

"Oh yes," said the waitress, sitting down with them, "my cousin's wife's sisters's son saw it, clear as the nose on your face."

"Could we talk to him?" demanded Frank. "I'm really interested in monsters."

"You're Frank N. Stein aren't you? I saw you and your wee monster on television. I'm really sorry to hear he's disappeared."

"We're trying to find him," Frank told her, "and any help your cousin's wife's sister's son could give us would be very useful."

"Do you think he's up here then, your Steinasaurus Rex? Well now, maybe he's courting our Nessie. Is that what you think?"

"We don't know," said Mr Stein, "but it does seem a bit of a coincidence that Nessie is active again just when our monster goes missing."

"True," said the waitress beginning to get really interested.

"Have any strangers come to the area recently?" asked Frank.

"Och hen, there are always strangers coming here," replied the waitress. "This is a tourist area."

"Hmmm," said Mrs Stein. "I think we need to let people know that we are here. Then anyone with any information can get in touch."

"My husband's mother's brother's third cousin by marriage runs the local paper, should I give him a wee ring?"

"Please," chorused the Steins.

The next day the headline in the local paper read: "Is Steinasaurus Rex stalking Scotland?" and there was a big picture of Frank and his parents.

"Good," said Mrs Stein, "Let's see if that brings in any information."

Just then the phone rang and they were asked to be on local radio and television.

"This is going just as I planned it," said Mr Stein, smiling. "Come on, let's go and tell as many people as possible that we are here."

That evening they had supper at the hotel. During the meal the hotel manager came in to say that there was a phone call for Frank – no one else would do. Frank went and answered the call.

"Frank N. Stein here. Can I help you?"

"No," came a girl's voice, "but I can help you. I know where your monster is."

"What? Why? Where is he? Are you sure it's him?" asked Frank sharply.

"All he does is call out 'Frank' over and over again. It must be your monster. Please, please won't you come straight away?"

"You bet I will," said Frank firmly. "Tell me where to come and I'll be there."

"I'm in Glen Gordon Castle," said the girl. "It's a bit of a way above the loch."

"Is that the castle I can see from the window?" asked Frank.

"That's the one."

"But we were told the owner was away and it was empty."

"That's what they want people to think, but it's not true – there are a lot of people here and they're keeping your monster a prisoner. My name's Morag. You'll know me by my bright red hair. Take care, Frank, these people are dangerous."

"OK Morag. I'll be there as fast as I can."

Found?

Frank walked back to his parents with a determined look on his face.

"I think I've tracked him down. I've just had tip-off from a girl whose mother is the house keeper, up there, at the castle."

"So what did this girl actually say?" asked Mr Stein.

"She says my monster is being kept prisoner there. She wanted me to go and meet her, and I've promised to go alone."

"I don't like the sound of that," interrupted his mother. "Who knows what kind of people we're dealing with here."

"I couldn't agree more," said Mr Stein frowning and looking worried. "I think we should tell the police immediately."

"No Dad," said Frank. "I promised. I promised that girl. . . and anyway who knows what they might do to my poor monster if the police turnd up. No, I have to go alone."

"I'm not happy about it," said Mrs Stein.

"Me neither," agreed her husband, putting his arm around her.

"Well you know where I'm going," said Frank pointing up the hill.

"And if you're not back in one hour we'll send the police in, promise or no promise," said Mr Stein firmly.

"Fair enough," said Frank. He raced out of the hotel and ran even faster up the hill and out of sight.

As he was running along Frank heard a car and looked up. It was a taxi. He flagged it down and jumped in.

"To the castle," he panted, "as fast as you can!"

"Are you the laddie that lost his monster?" asked the cab driver.

"Yes," said Frank. "Do you know anything about him."

"Well, I'm not sure if I do or not. I was driving some people home the other night and I saw a huge creature wandering over the mountains, banging his chest and yelling something like, 'Thanks, thanks!' My wife says I must have been drinking."

"Did you tell the police?" asked Frank.

"I did not. People are always reporting monsters here, the police get sick of it."

"So if you wanted to imprison a monster, Loch Ness would be a good place to do it?"

"Aye, that could be right. But who would want to imprison a monster, young man?"

"I don't know, but that is precisely what

I'm hoping to find out," Frank told him. "Stop! Stop here please, I need to get out."

"I can't leave you here, laddie, all on your own on a deserted road. Let me take your right up to the castle."

"No, no thank you. This is fine."

"I'll just wait here a wee moment and see that you're all right."

"No, no please don't. I need to be alone."

"Well OK, if that's what you want. But I'm not too happy about it."

Frank watched as the cab drove away down the hill. It was getting dark, he began to feel nervous.

Suddenly he heard the crunch of footsteps on gravel. Frank's heart raced as he ran and hid behind a rock.

"It's all right Frank," came a voice. "It's only me – Morag." A girl with bright red curls jumped down next to him.

"Hello," said Frank, holding his hand out formally.

"Hi," said Morag.

"Can you tell me what's going on?" asked Frank.

"Not really because I don't understand myself," she replied.

"They've got your monster locked up in the castle. He was in chains at first."

"And he ate them?" said Frank smiling.

"I think so," agreed the girl smiling back.

"But why do they want my monster?"

"I told you, I don't know. I think they want him to eat something."

"My monster eats anything," Frank told her. "Why would anyone want to kidnap him just for that?"

"I don't understand it and neither does your monster."

"Have you talked to him?"

"Yes, I was so sorry for him. But all he could tell me was that they wanted him to eat something but he's not hungry because he misses you. So all he does is cry and say he wants his boy Frank. That's why I helped him escape."

"Escape!"

"Yes, I unlocked the door of the cell while those horrible men were watching television. He ran away but they caught up with him pretty quickly."

"My poor monster," cried Frank. "Why didn't you tell anyone about him?"

"My mum said I was to keep quiet, she's worried about her job. After I stole the key of the monsters cell, she thought she would get into trouble. She's been unemployed for years you see. But I phoned the paper with that story about the Loch Ness Monster I thought it would give you a clue."

"It was a great idea," said Frank, "and it certainly worked. Mum and Dad insisted we get here straightaway."

"I know, and I was going to leave it to you after that, but the monster is so miserable. He won't eat a thing and I couldn't bear it any more. . . so in the end I rang you up."

"You're great, Morag. Steinasaurus Rex and I will never be able to repay you."

"We'll worry about that after we rescue him. Come on! Let's go and see exactly what's going on in the castle."

To The Rescue!

Frank and Morag climbed up the slopes to the castle. Morag quietly opened the back door and Frank followed her upstairs. As they got nearer the heart of the castle they heard great sighs and sobs.

"Frank, I want my boy Frank!"a voice moaned.

"My poor monster," thought Frank, trying hard not to cry.

Then they heard, "Take it away. I don't want to eat anything – not until you bring my boy here."

"I wish we could get our hands on that Frank N. Stein," came a man's angry voice. "Maybe he would get this stupid monster to eat and then we could all get out of here."

"I don't like being here anymore than

you do but we agreed to get rid of this nuclear waste and get rid of it we will," said another man's voice.

"Yeah, he's got to eat it. I mean, we're sitting on a gold mine. We could get nuclear waste from all over the world."

"I know. . . just think, no one knows what to do with the stuff – they'd pay us any money to get it off their hands. We'll be rich. Sooner or later this brute will get hungry and do our work for us, don't you worry."

Frank had frozen with horror.

"Nuclear waste, they want my poor monster to eat nuclear waste!" he cried.

"Come on, Steinasaurus," said one of the men. "Eat this up and you can go free, you can go back to your boy."

"Yeah," said the other voice. "You must be getting very hungry. It's days since you ate. Come on – have a nice little snack now and then maybe a proper big supper later."

"Do you promise that I can see my boy if I eat this?"

"We do."

"Cross your hearts and hope to die?"

"Cross our hearts and hope to die."

"Oh all right then, give it here. You're right I am bit peckish."

At that moment Frank burst in through the door, "No! Don't Steinasaurus Rex! Don't even take a little bite."

"Frank, my boy Frank!" cried the monster, breaking into a huge smile.

"Put me down Steinasaurus," yelled Frank. "This is very serious."

"I'm that pleased to see you, my boy Frank. I'll just eat what these men want me to eat and then we can go home."

"No!" screamed Frank "Don't touch it."

"Come on, Frank, I'm hungry. I missed my boy so much I didn't eat a thing. But now you're here I feel like my old self again and I'm starving."

The monster picked up one of the metal canisters with a skull and cross bones on it.

"Look!" yelled Frank, "That sign means what's inside is poisonous."

"Not to a monster," said one of the men.

"That's right," agreed the monster, lifting the canister to his mouth.

"No, put it down!" yelled Frank at the top of his voice. "If you eat that you will never be able to live near me or any other person. Put it down, please put it down!"

The monster dropped the canister on the the floor. It fell with a thud on the foot of one of the kidnappers. He jumped up and down yelling in pain.

"Now why would that be Frank? Why wouldn't you want to be my friend if I ate this stuff?"

"Because it's radio-active monster. People get very ill if they come into contact with radio-active material. Everyone would run away from you."

"Even you, my boy Frank?"

"Yes, even me."

The monster glared at his kidnappers. "You wanted me to eat something that would mean I could never be near my boy Frank. That makes me very cross."

The monster thumped his chest angrily
and ran towards the two men. They went
white with terror and raced to the door.

The monster followed them shouting
and shrieking.

"I'll get you for trying to make me eat
that stuff. Just you wait!"

"No, Steinasaurus, come back," called
Frank.

But the monster took no notice. He chased the men down the stairs and through the kitchens out into the castle grounds, shouting "Wait till I get you! I'll munch and crunch you, oh yes I will!"

The two men ran over the drawbridge but when they saw the police coming towards them, they turned and ran back again. They were trapped between the monster, and the police and Mr and Mrs Stein. They decided there was only one thing to do. They jumped off the drawbridge and into the moat. The monster jumped in after them and they scrambled up the other bank into the arms of the police.

"Save us," they shouted "We surrender, the monster is after us. We confess, we admit everything. We did it all, we'll answer all your questions, just save us from Steinasaurus Rex!"

"Get them into the van quickly," said the police chief, as the monster charged towards them yelling.

"I'll get you. . . trying to separate me from my boy. You just wait till I catch up with you. There'll be some crunching done!"

The two men cowered in the back of the police van.

"Drive on!"' instructed the police chief. "Get them out of here."

"Where's Frank?" demanded Mrs Stein. "Is he all right, where's my son?"

"I'm here mum, I'm fine," called Frank, as he ran panting out of the building, followed by Morag. "This is my friend Morag, she helped me find my monster. Her mum works in the castle and Morag heard Steinasaurus crying. It was Morag who got the rumours going about Nessie."

"Congratulations Morag, and thank you very much," cried Mr Stein.

Mrs Stein gave the monster a big hug. "Glad to see you Steinasaurus Rex, we've all been so worried."

"What was going on in the castle?" asked the police chief.

"Those men kidnapped my monster. They planned to make their fortunes by getting my monster to eat all of the nuclear waste that people don't know what do with."

"Nuclear waste! That is serious, is it in the castle?"

"Yes," said Frank "And my monster nearly ate it because he didn't understand."

"Call in some back-up," snapped the police chief into his radio. "There's nuclear waste in that castle. No-one is to be allowed in. Get the government to take it away. No one else is to touch it."

He turned to the Steins "Those kidnappers will be up on a serious charge," he told them. "Illegally disposing of nuclear waste, why that could kill thousands of people. Trying to get your monster to eat it indeed."

"Talking about eating," said the

monster,"I'm very hungry. I haven't eaten for over a week."

And he went over to a police car and ate it in two gulps.

"That's better," he said grinning at the horrified group. "Now I'm back with my boy Frank and I'm not hungry anymore, what more could monster want?"

The Steins looked at each other in horror.

"Sorry about the car," mumbled Mr Stein, "he only does that when he's very hungry indeed."

"I should hope so! I've never seen anything like it in my life," said the Police Chief. "Still, it's a small price to pay to catch villains who are messing around with nuclear waste. Well done, Frank, for helping catch them. Now excuse me a minute while I sort out a wee problem."

The Police Chief picked up his radio again and said, "Send a large lorry round here quickly, and I mean yesterday. Destination the municipal rubbish dump!"